He had already polished off a slice of steak, half a ham and a whole string of sausages.

"What can I eat next?" he wondered.

At last, he came to a town.

It was market day, and the streets bustled with busy shoppers and bright stalls.

Dog sniffed. Something, somewhere smelled delicious.

What can it be?

The Grasshopper

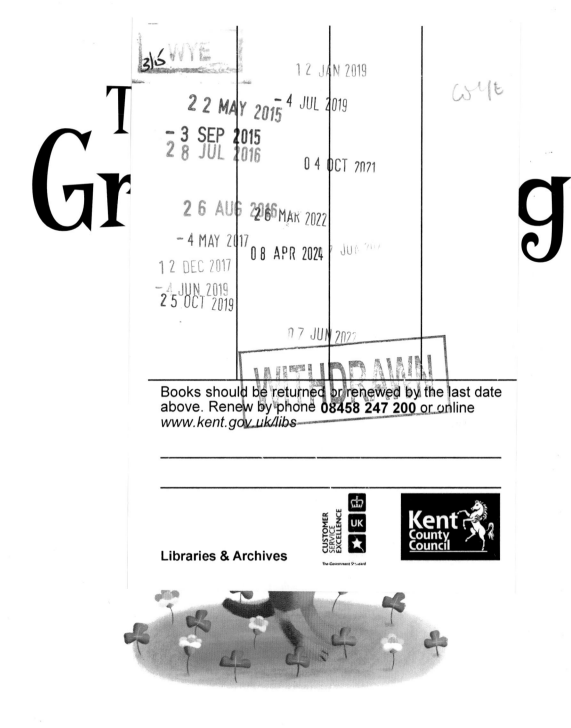

Based on a story by Aesop
Retold by Rosie Dickins

Dog was padding along,
dreaming about dinner.

Mmmm...

"Ooh, look at that big, juicy bone!" he drooled. He could almost taste it already.

"I've **got** to have it!"

The butcher was busy selling sausages.
No one noticed greedy Dog.

Slowly,
  silently,
    he crept
      closer...

    and closer.

Hey!

Snap!
His teeth closed
around the bone.

And he bounded
away before anyone
could stop him.

Soon, the town
was far behind.

I'm so clever!

Dog wagged his tail with delight.

"Now I have my bone to eat," he thought.
"I just need something to drink."

His path ran past
a rippling river.

"That water
looks good,"
thought Dog.

Dog padded over to the water's edge.
He peered down...

and saw another dog
gazing back at him.

What was more,
the other dog
had a bone too!

"His bone is bigger than mine,"
thought Dog crossly.

"It's not fair! **His** bone looks so big and juicy."

"I've **got** to have it!

Now, how can I make him drop it?"

Dog bared his sharp, white teeth
and let out a fearsome growl.

The dog in the water growled too.

Grrr!

Dog didn't give up.
He raised his hackles and
barked furiously.

WOOF!

WOOF!

WOOF!

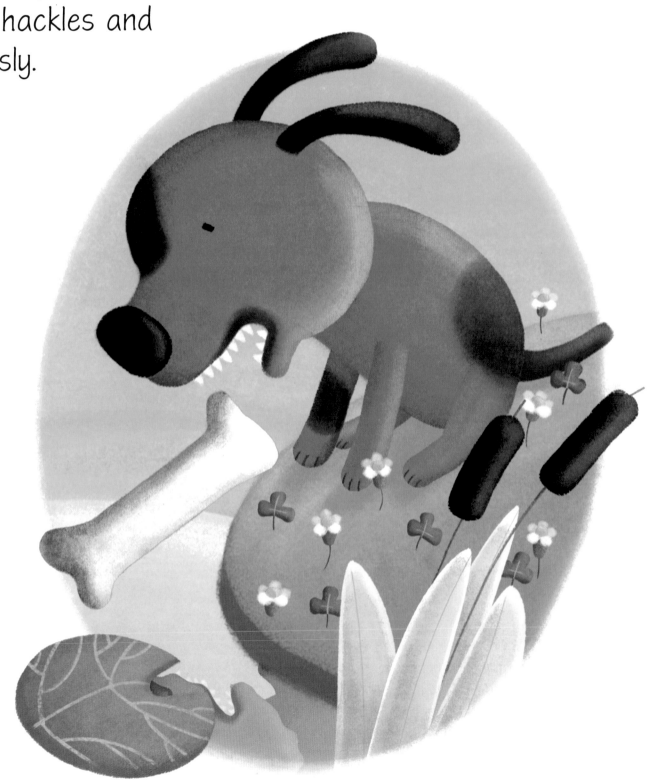

"Uh-oh!" His big, beautiful bone dropped out of his mouth and fell...

Splosh!

into the river.

Ripples spread across the surface.

The other dog vanished...

and so did Dog's bone.

"Nooo!" whined Dog. He reached after it, but the water was too deep.

Now I have nothing.

His bone had sunk without a trace.

Too late Dog realized...
there was no dog in the water.

And there was
no other bone.

He had been jealous of his own reflection!

"Silly me," he sighed.

"I should have been
happy with what I had."

About the story

People think this story was written about 2,500 years ago by an Ancient Greek man named Aesop. He told many stories about animals, always ending with a 'moral' or lesson about how to behave.

Edited by Lesley Sims
Designed by Laura Wood
Additional design by Louise Bartlett

This edition first published in 2015 by Usborne Publishing Ltd., Usborne House,
83-85 Saffron Hill, London EC1N 8RT, England. www.usborne.com
Copyright © 2015, 2007 Usborne Publishing Ltd.